MORE THAN JUST A SHADOW

Collection of Poems

BY

REA MAAC

Copyright © 2021 MORE THAN JUST A SHADOW by Rea Maac

Published by Poetry Planet Book Publishing House
Designed and arranged by Tess Ritumalta
Edited by Marie Ezekiel
Please submit all reviews and comments or report errors to maac.iyah20@gmail.com.

Illustrations are used courtesy of Pinterest and Pixabay and may contain their own copywrites.

ISBN:
Softbound: 978-621-8261-15-0
Hardbound: 978-621-8261-13-6
Mobile/Kindle: 978-621-8261-14-3

DEDICATION

This book is dedicated to my parents for always loving and supporting me despite my shortcoming. To my siblings for always being ready to raise my name every time I achieve something extraordinary. To Yroll, the key to my success, and to Jan for the undying support since day one. I also dedicate this book to those who encouraged me to fly towards my dreams.

ACKNOWLEDGEMENT

I would like to express my special thanks of gratitude to Poetry Planet Publishing house for opening their door and building the bridge for me to reach my dreams.

Special gratitude is also given to my family for always being there who believe in my capabilities and to all the people around me who always there to encourage me to keep soaring high and never give up on my passion for writing.

PREFACE

Someone asked me, how do I write poems?

I said, I took my heart and sprinkled it in every word of my poem. When I cannot scream the truth in my head and the bottled emotions in my heart, that's when my pen does the job by tattooing all of them on a piece of paper. Being a migrant, living alone, miles apart from my family, the pen has been there all the time to encode my thoughts. When my ink dries up, I noticed all the shadows of my past, but if you will open your heart while reading every piece of this book, you will realize that this book is more than just a shadow of my life experiences. The lessons I learned, the strength I gained after facing all the challenges, how I managed to pick up all the pieces of my broken heart and how I composed myself to stand up and start anew after falling so many times; I can say that my book is "More Than Just A Shadow". Behind this book are all the people who serve as

my inspiration to keep on going despite failures for me to achieve my dreams.

This book is a medley of my sufferings, happiness, contentment, fear, pain, anger, trust, uncertainty, love, heartaches, and observations in society. Every piece is a window into my heart and tells an important story.

These poems are not just a collection of all my written pieces; compiled together, this is where my heart is!

The author

TABLE OF CONTENTS

Copyright © 2021 MORE THAN JUST A SHADOW by Rea Maac 2

DEDICATION 3

ACKNOWLEDGEMENT 4

PREFACE 5

TABLE OF CONTENTS 7

BELIEVE ME OR NOT 11

WOMAN'S HAND 12

EXTRAORDINARY 14

ODE TO MY PARENTS 16

INITIATION 18

IS IT SOMETHING TO BE PROUD OF? 19

I AM HERE 21

RECLAMATION OF CHICKEN WAY OF LIVING 24

REAL/REEL 26

ELEGY FOR MY FUTURE SELF 28

LOVE CONQUERS ALL 30

I WONDER WHY 32

LIFT ME UP 34

STEPS 36

SCARECROW 37

LIFE IS A RIDE 39

AM NOT GOING AWAY 41

LOCKDOWN PILLS 44

VOICE OF LESS FORTUNATE 45

HELLO 48

SPECIAL TREATMENT 49

IF I CAN 53

EMPTINESS 55

WHEN X=0 56

HEARTBEAT 57

BATAM 58

LET ME TRAVEL WITH THE WATER 60

FOR THE BEST DAD 62

SHADOW 63

KING OF EVIL 66

STAGNANT WATER 69

A MAN IN MY DREAMS 70

ROAD TO INFINITY 72

BLESSING OF NEW YEAR 73

DUST 74

KEY OF HAPPINESS 76

SO NEAR 78

I DO 79

NOTHING 80

BEHIND MASK...81

UNICO IJO..83

TOGETHER FOREVER 84

HOLLOW 87

EMPAT PERKATAAN...88

DAYDREAMING...89

COME AND GO...92

FIGHTING SPIRIT 94

TWO FACES OF MIGRANT'S LIFE.......................96

TREAT OR TRICK 98

NUCLEUS POEMS 99

WHEN HEAVENS WEPT...100

I RIDE...101

WHEN I CAN'T USE "E" 102

AFTER A DECADE..104

FORGIVE ME...106

WHISPER OF THE MIND 110

ABOUT THE AUTHOR 113

BELIEVE ME OR NOT

I am not a good writer

And I know it is not true that

I have my talent

For I am sure

My writings are bland

So don't insist that

I can write poems with good rhymes

I can compose a concrete one

Because every single day I believe that

I always have grammatical mistakes

I don't care even if you admit that

I am good in Volta

You liked my twin cinema

You enjoyed my imagery

You surprised by my metaphor

I know deep down my heart

My effort is not enough

So don't say that

I am a good poet!

(Now read from bottom to top)

WOMAN'S HAND

Etched with our dreams

Began to love measuring our patience

Mending patches

Cutting out negativities

Picking up broken pieces

Turn clipping into a masterpiece

Refuse to surrender when things go wrong

Start all over no matter if it takes so long

Learning how to adjust the tension

Minding side by side without pretension

Touching every corner if you need any correction

Delivering the final draft with perfection

These hands lead us in the right direction

Leading us to achieve our passion

Imagine this woman's hand

Imagine your hands, imagine their hands

Imagine a million hands

Who guide one another

Who helps each other

Who works together

Can you grasp a thought

 how amazing our future is?

EXTRAORDINARY

She was shipwrecked into a society

that tried to stitch her lips, snatched her voice,

But she knew she wasn't born

to keep her mouth shut,

She wasn't born to stay inside

 the four corner of her room

She was born to shine,

to speak up

to walk on her chosen path

to enrich her talent that lies within

To follow her heart,

filled with compassion inside

So there she is, standing up!

A woman with a heart full of love

With patience, she strives

Rearing other people's child

Showering them with love and care

Treated like her own

With full of hope

Homesickness she can cope

A woman, an inspiration

For her courage and determination

Who always keeps her head up high

Like a bird soaring in the sky

Surrounded by people who sculpting her image

She was there, serving with passion

She was there, doing a good deed

Letting it shine over the horizon to be counted

 and remember in the society

 that punched her below the belt.

She is far from what they wanted her to be

She has her own capacity

She has her own standard of beauty

With her unending story

She is extraordinary.

ODE TO MY PARENTS

With love and care, you enveloped me

In your arms with warmth and safety.

You have always wiped away,

my agitation, my hidden blubbering.

 As I grow old you have nurtured me

to be a better version of myself

You lead the way and thought me

 how to measure the right scales of life

You set an example and showed me

how to curl if the blanket is short.

I was born without a silver spoon

And I wasn't raised in a mansion

Yet I was showered with so much love

A love that was depth and wide like an ocean

though sometimes it irritates my eyes, still

I chose to soak myself in you over and over.

When you hold my hands I can feel

your love in the roughness of your hands

Turning night into day

To support me all the way

Despite my shortcomings

Your care remain humming

My dearest mother and father

I love you and thank you for always being there

The joy of being your daughter

Is the best gift that I will treasure forever?

INITIATION

Hour upon hour

I tried to fight

But I can't do it right

One step forward

One step backward

My legs are aching

My bones are twisting

Pain unrivaled!

Driving me insane!

Caught in the undertow of the wave

So let me go through the dark cave

Until I pass the test.

IS IT SOMETHING TO BE PROUD OF?

I am a bad mother

And I refuse to believe that

I can raise my son alone

I realize that I am still young but

Here I am, I will be successful

Is a lie.

I am a failure

My past defines my future.

It's not true that

I can stand up again while facing hurdles

I can still make difference despite barriers

Because the truth is

I don't deserve a second chance.

I don't believe that

There's a strength inside of me.

Let me tell you this:

I may be still young but

We were wrong

Both of us surely enjoyed but

He has no backbone

He left me during pregnancy

People knew

I am an irresponsible mother

I don't agree that

A single mom is an incredible human.

(Now read from bottom to top)

I AM HERE

Alone

Trapped in the closed wall of my anxiety

Isolated, screaming silently

Perhaps you never notice

Maybe because I am not eye-catching

Like a Mercedes-Benz

I am not appealing like Coach and Chanel

I don't have the scent of Burberry

There's no Swarovski in my body.

I am up here

In one of the units of the high-rise building

Perhaps you're too busy

To see me

Maybe because I portray an imperfection

My crumpled skin is a sign of an expiration

Waiting for my day to fall

The moment of my final call

To have a peaceful soul.

I am here

Searching for a familiar face,

I am here

calling your name

I am here

pleading for help

But you never answer

Perhaps you didn't hear

Perhaps you chose not to care.

RECLAMATION OF CHICKEN WAY OF LIVING

I am living from hand to mouth

 For I am less fortunate

For I wasn't born with a golden spoon in my mouth

For I mostly eat rice with water and salt

For I don't have a concrete bungalow, just a simple nipa hut

For I am not well-educated and not smart

For I did not study in a prestigious school

For I don't have an i-phone

For I am an old-fashion

For I don't wear those branded clothes instead I have a second-hand

For what I earn in a day just enough on that certain day

For I have to turns night into day to be able to survive

For I have to scratch a foreign soil to find a piece of food

For I believe this is an effective method

If this is the way I can lift my dreams

I am proud to be compared to a chicken

For after the hard work and pain success I will gain.

REAL/REEL

I am a bad influence

I cannot say that

My friends love to hang out with me

Because I know

They are not one call away

It's not right to say

They will still accept me for who I am

Even if I had caused them pain in the past

And

They will remember me

For all the bad and not the good one

It's not true that

I have a positive impact

To my friends

Here's the truth:

I encourage them to help others

Is a lie

I push them to lie to their parents

Because no matter what they said

I don't lead people to the right way

So don't insist that

I cared.

27

(read from bottom to top)

ELEGY FOR MY FUTURE SELF

While my fragrance still hanging
in the air, whispering forgiveness
I hope you've been happy by the time
you finally close your eyes
 and your breath bid goodbye.

In between your success and failure
In between your tears and laughter
In between your heartbreaks
With all your dreams and choices
that made you stronger than ever
I hope you have been happy at least.
May all the love you gave away
will return to you upon seeing you
beautiful in white, lying in peace.

I wonder, how many loved ones
will shed tears once they hear
the news that you are forever
gone. Those days that you lighted up
their dark paths, will they light yours

as you walk down the aisle

to bless one last time.

Forgive me for all the wrong

Forgive me for being harsh

I hope you can still align

the road that I took

I hope all my wrong, you

can still make it right.

If you can burn those mistake

of your yesterday, I wish you will

turn them into ashes, or bury at least

together with you.

Forgive me for being me

Forgive me for being so unselfish,

that I have left you nothing

 but a grave of peace

and a soul of happiness.

LOVE CONQUERS ALL

If we think love will last even after the rain

Our hearts will never let go

It will withstand every pain

We will not let promises hang in vain

We will face the storm, together we will grow

If we think love will last even after the rain

Fights after fights, love will remain

No matter what the future will show

It will withstand every pain

Tears may spill, but we will wipe the stain

We will always a lover not a foe

If we think love will last even after the rain

There will/ have many reasons to complain

But our love is like a raging sea, so

It will withstand every pain

I will love you again and again

Till death do us part forever me and you

If we think love will last after the rain

It will withstand every pain.

I WONDER WHY

While darkness glazing the world silently,

I saw the moon seems to stare back at me.

The clouds passing by as if saying hi

And those bed of stars twinkling in the sky.

Here I am tossing myself in my bed.

Trying to erase some thoughts in my head.

In love, do we have to suffer?

Is that how it works to find forever?

I witnessed how you love him like a king.

You said you'll never let go of the string.

He said his heart only belongs to you.

Always vow he will not make you feel blue.

He said you're the only one in his heart.

Yet he repeatedly tore it apart.

Leakage of salted water, you embrace

when venom of love attack and takes place.

Is there any antidote to get rid

of the poison that swollen our eyelid?

You keep forgiving him as if it's fine

I wonder why you never draw a line.

Why do you let your trust stained by lies?

Why do you let those dust tainted our eyes?

Unlike the moon being tainted by the cloud,

we have choices, a mind to think out loud.

Here I am still wide awake wondering

Why love gave the most intricate feeling?

LIFT ME UP
(Something I need to hear)

And God wept that it hurt you so;

But it was allowed to shape you.

Courage helps you grow.

Dance with it, accept without no.

Everything has a reason, it's not

Faith, nor coincidence.

God has planned your existence.

He's in control, mind your patience.

I saw you fight but don't let

jealousy destroy your mind; be

kind. Don't be greedy.

Love unselfishly.

Mend what is broken

Never hate too long

Offer and seek forgiveness

Pray always.

Quality or quantity of friends

Revise carefully

Select those necessary;

Treat them nicely.

Understand yourself

Value your talent; don't

Waste your time

X-factor is in your hands.

Yeah, pull it out; your

Zeal for poetry.

STEPS

It's all about the steps

Not the top of the stairs

Because every step I take

Is an opportunity to win the race

It brings new light to strive

No matter what I will survive

Sometimes I lose, sometimes I gain

Sometimes I was caught between joy and pain

But every step is a reflection

It's a mirror that brings a new lesson

To keep me going on

Every step is a declaration

That I can reach my destination.

SCARECROW

There was a scarecrow

in the middle of the crowd

standing alone in silence

because no one notices its presence.

The mouth was kept shut

piercing cries echoing in its mind

trying to be heard

but the voice has lost its purpose.

You think it's nothing

Only a figure to scare away birds

it's more than that

if only you'll open your heart.

You can hear the pleading

but you choose not to listen

you can see its suffering

but you were blindfolded by arrogance.

Staying quiet, forever alone

speaking may lose a battle

afraid of the outcome.

Pity for the scarecrow

might be thrown after being used

without a single compliment

to its undying effort.

In the affluent crowd

being manipulated by the selfish act

I know because I'm

the scarecrow in a foreign land.

(This poem was included in CALL AND RESPONSE: Local and Migrant Anthology)

LIFE IS A RIDE

Our life,

 just like a bicycle

  We have to focus

in balance

Each hand

 manage the handle well

Once fall,

still have a chance.

Enjoy the ride,

  keep on moving

 Along the path

 you may be see

Those obstacles

   and bad things

 That will cause you

    to stop the journey.

 They might hurt you,

but pick them up

Never surrender,

    always move forward

Remember

    to reach on top

You have to fight

    no matter what.

AM NOT GOING AWAY

Am I walking in the wrong way

And you'll do a virtuous play?

Climbing up a rocky mountain

will push my soul into pain

But am not going away

Tomorrow may rain

Word of honour in vain

But am not going away

Alarm is ringing

Brain is calling

Music is playing

But am not going away

So many dark clouds unfold

So many thoughts untold

So much word to say

But am not going away

I would like to stay.

I will stay.

(poem without E)

LOCKDOWN PILLS

To be taken within 2 months

Proprietary blend:

Eating with 20g sadness, working with 30g tears

sleeping with 100g prayer, a 100g of hope

Nutritional values: 100% self-realization

Expiration: 1 June 2020

Important notice: to be taken seriously, follow the
instruction correctly

Side effect: no rest day

VOICE OF LESS FORTUNATE

I chose to leave my country
to change my destiny
here in a city full of gold
 arrived with only hope
dream in my pocket
hoping for a better future
seeking for a greener pasture

everything goes smoothly
but suddenly I found myself
 in the cage of uncertainties,
my soul was wrapped in fears
the night covered with tears
and to the cold breeze, I whispered
"where do I go from here?"

the enemy is hiding in the dark
in silence, I was attacked
cries of desperation echoed
Loss of life is inevitable
tomorrow still untold

sphere stabbing my heart

I am craving

my family is waiting

my son is longing

but what's more painful

when they clinch their fists

full of insult, point their nimble

fingers to my colour,

smashed me with hated looks,

 I am sorry

for being added to the list

I didn't ask for it

 I was isolated

can't clean your bins

can't wash your drains

I am sorry

 if I can't answer

when you call my name

I can't be there

I am sorry

if I have to rest

fighting at my best

alone here

I am fighting

not as a suspect but

a victim of misjudgment.

HELLO

Ma, did I make you worry?

For not calling you weekly

If that so, I'm sorry

I didn't do it intentionally

Just quite busy

Work wasn't easy

But rest assured, I can handle it properly.

Ma, don't you worry about me

Everything will be alright, I guarantee

I'm waiting for the day to cross the sea

To feel the love you have for me

To see your smile and eat your delicacy

To chat with you while having a cup of coffee

One day I will be back to hug you tightly

And stay by your side permanently

Ma, I miss you tremendously.

SPECIAL TREATMENT

You told her, she's stupid

while pointing a finger at her face.

You're not happy seeing your maid

Still wiping your car window shield

"Quick" you firmly said!

What a nice breakfast meal

For your maid who is standing still.

Yet she remains humble

while your mouth grumbles.

The hot iron is not meant to grill

 Her body is already ill

She's not Rapunzel, why pulling her hair?

Stomping her on the ground

A toy in her, you found.

You slapped her...

You kicked her...

You punched her...

Beating her to release your anger

To show that you're the master

You gave her cold leftover

Or sliced bread soaked in water

Yet you still have the guts to complain

Your house is not well-maintain.

Tormented at a young age

Just like a bird inside the cage

She wanted to escape and soar high

But unable to fly

She was approached by many

Pleading for her safety

But it's too late, she already lost her sanity

In just a blink, people were screaming

She jumped off the building

She committed suicide.

Lying in blood, she died.

I don't know how should I start

Those feelings shouting from my heart

Recalling yesterday's footprints and scars was hard

Where to begin and how to end

I don't know if I will be heard.

So I chose to use paper and ink

To scribble hope that was clear and succinct

Hope that was seems denied to someone like me

Someone like me who is a maid.

To be called maid is nothing

but to be called stupid how does it feel?

Have you tried it? How was it?

Does it taste sweet like chocolate?

Do you know that your words

are sharp like a knife chopping her whole being

Like a fire that burns her feeling?

We're here fighting unseen battles

To achieve our dreams

We came here to work and earn money

Seeking a greener pasture for our family

We came here to live not to be tortured mentally

Not to abused emotionally

Not to be hurt physically

We came here to earn a living

Not to stop us from breathing

We came here full of hope

Not to endure excruciating pain

Not to be sent home inside the coffin.

We are not perfect,

We make mistakes

We are not highly educated,

 Our service was paid

But is it enough to implement their fist?

We are also a human

 but where is the treatment of humanity?

IF I CAN

If I could I would fly in the sky

Like a bird, to tour around the earth

I will sprinkle love and fill the world with God's
word

Wipe away the pain, tears, and fear

Heal the broken heart, teach people to be real.

I will find the truth behind the lies

To determine who is in disguise.

To watch and catch all the thief,

Fill their heart with goodwill

Pulling them out of the dark

 and have a new start

Pray for them not to go astray again.

If I could turn back time I would

Be a kid lying in the crib

Nothing matters but milk and bib.

To feel and hear my parents' touch and hymn.

To let them carry me and dance in the air.

To sleep, putting my head over my father's feet

Life seems easy when we're still a baby.

If only I could I would.

If only I could.

If only.

EMPTINESS

I've been trying to trace your whereabouts

 but everywhere I go, I couldn't find you.

I went to the shore to look for a left-over fragrance,
hoping for a footprints

 of our memories in the past but there's

 nothing, totally faded,

what's left were those coral brought by the waves

which seemed unknown to my heart.

I'm in the middle of the dark

standing alone, feeling hungry,

like an owl waiting for prey to arrive.

I wonder why, why did you have to leave me?

Our memories that I treasured

like gold, left me when I need them the most.

From the day you run away from me

my heart has been void and unattended.

WHEN X=0

stop asking the value of X

You can always change variables

and don't ask Y

HEARTBEAT

in just a blink

you disappeared

there's nothing left

but the story

inside of her

bulging belly

BATAM

If you're escaping from Lion City

Just a quick ride in a ferry

Mere 45 minutes of the journey

To reach the fancy island seems easy

Like Los Angeles Hollywood

Batam has its Hollywood-esque

A sign "Welcome to Batam"

Satu, dua, tiga, ready...selfie

When she arrived, she was mesmerized

Wonderful place in front of her eyes

Awesome attraction, stunning beaches

A better place if you're looking for peace

At Golden Prawn 555 Kelong

What she really like is a steamed *gonggong*

Generous amount of seafood, she was surprised

Sumptuous lunch at an affordable price

One thing she keeps insisting

She swears I will not regret

It is a must to buy *Kueh Lapis*

Which was called a Layered cake in English.

Should I visit this place, *sayah tidak tahu*

What's the meaning, I don't know.

To a friend of mine, kudos to you

Terimah Kasih for sharing an info.

LET ME TRAVEL WITH THE WATER

I went to the shore to watch the waves

The water seems to invite me to touch them

I run my finger through the water and I shivered

I wonder if the water can understand me...

If the water can feel the pain inside me

I stepped into the water to feel the coolness

I wish I could float on the water

And let it carry me anywhere and everywhere

It goes, anywhere and everywhere without
stopping

Anywhere and everywhere just keep on moving

Like how I wanted to run away from the people

Who broke my heart and caused me pain

I wanted to float on the water

And let it teach me how to travel anywhere

Let it carry me and keep moving forward

Without turning back.

FOR THE BEST DAD

In this world, no one can erase his love

Because his love already engraved in my heart

He's the best gift I received from above

And I miss him, now that we're far apart.

From the day I was born until now

To love and support us is his only vow

To do whatever it takes

To give whatever we need.

Though his hand and legs already shaken

His love will never be mistaken.

He's the only man who will never hurt me

The only man who will not break my heart

The only man who will cater to my every wish

The only man who knows me best.

He is the tree I lay upon

Whenever my knees pull me down

He is the star in the night

That serves as my light.

SHADOW

I woke up in the middle of the night,

I couldn't find the source of my light.

I buried my face in my pillow,

trying to avoid those shadows

that keeps haunting my ego.

After swallowing my pride I took a stride.

I went to the garden and searched

 for his left-over fragrance, but there's nothing else

 aside from the dried leaves

 scattered in the surface.

Actually, we're on good terms,

We found companionship amidst

the hunger for a greener pasture.

We were so eager to win the race

We were both aiming for the ace

You see...

We traveled across the sea

We dug the foreign land

To have the prize in our hand.

But our world turned upside down

He runs so fast, I am slower

And that makes him angry

He didn't notice...

I can barely walk because I was carrying his loads

I can barely walk due to my swollen toes

when he accidentally steps on my shoes.

I called him to come back to me

To give me a hand, so I can walk a bit easy

But he pushed me away instead

I am too heavy to carry, he said.

Running without me made it easy for him,

he reached the top of the mountain

holding the flag, screaming he's the winner.

I gave him a round of applause

 before I realized that I was there

at the cliff, hanging...

Bleeding.

I fell down on my own blood.

Likewise, I went back to our cage

Waited for him to embrace,

cooked his favourite dishes

He arrived a bit late

I thought he'll give me a hug and kiss, but he took
his luggage instead

He said he has to leave to find himself.

I asked him to stay

Yet he didn't hear me anyway.

While salted water about to leak

He left.

KING OF EVIL

You may curious at first

Trying to conquer your thirst

To see how effective I can be

Am I going to bring satisfaction

Or simply destruction?

If you date me once I can still let you go

I can still push you away to save your ego

But if you stay with me twice or three

We will never break free

The sweats and shakes after every session

Your mind will be full of visions

I can make all your dreams come true

I can bring the best in you

I was told they are addicted to my scents

My charm they can't resists.

But before you date me

Let me tell you my story

I hate the following instruction

I love to lead the nation

I hate being taken for granted

I love to be praise

Though I live in luxury

I can still be with the poor

Even if I was born with a silver spoon

I can still live down the street

But let me warn you

I am not a game

Don't treat me like I am nothing

I am a king.

If I leave you, you'll get crazy

You'll despise everyone even your family

I can break you apart

And that's the start

You'll do everything just to be with me

And once you possess me

I'll own you completely

I will take everything from you

You'll give up everything

You'll give up your home

You'll give up your throne

You'll give up your money

You will be in debt

You will learn to steal

You will commit crimes

Just to feel the pleasure in my arms

I'll take and I'll take until

 the last drop of your conscience

Until you have nothing more to give.

I will be your king, you'll be my slave.

You'll be with me until your grave.

So please still not too late

Walk away, don't click the bait

If you care for your sanity

Don't dare touch me

If you love yourself and your family

Stay away from me

Stay away!

STAGNANT WATER

Years have gone by, but

nothing has changed, still

static in a savage space,

forgotten and unattended.

It has been alone, just

 hiding in the comfort zone;

Supposedly you must be there,

But you were gone,

you disappear.

It's been a long time since

 you've left, so quiet.

Mosquitoes took over

the place, algae scattered

on the surface.

A MAN IN MY DREAMS

I found myself thinking
 where you are, how far away
My idle mind and the tired heart
 waiting when will you arrive
Yearning and longing
 for your presence to embrace
When will be the time,
I could feel your caress
The days you left behind
 still hanging in the air,
Nothing has changed,
 still static and sluggish.

Spending most of the day
 wrapping myself with your leftover fragrance
And looking in every corner
to search for your trace.
I keep shifting your memories
 bit by bit every day
Reminiscing our moments together
to treat the loophole in any way.

Here I am drawing the moments

I am longing, dreaming

Because in my dreams

nobody is suffering

There are no tears flowing

There's no heart being broken.

In my dreams

No promises are hanging in vain

There's no selfish act from a villain.

In my dreams

There's no one controlling our decisions

That makes our hearts fall in contradiction.

In my dreams

There's no one twisting our mind

There's no pain being hidden.

My love, I'll just see you

in my dreams

because in my dreams,

we can conquer everything

and it was you and me

that matters in my dreams.

ROAD TO INFINITY

There in the middle of the farm.
Her castle standing with no harm.

She planned to build her family.
To live with peace and happily.

With him, who captured her shy heart.
Who promised the moon from the start.

They treat each other very well.
I can hear the ringing of a bell.

Although sometimes the weather is hot,
One of them took the ice, so fret not!

They always spend time together.
It looks like they have the same feather.

So can you pray and wish her luck?
That his heart will never be hacked.

BLESSING OF NEW YEAR

As I open my eyes
At exactly 6:00 in the morning
I heard the tickling sound
of the New Year's rain
It's so relaxing
Like a crystal clear going
 down my throat,
With the cold breeze
Peeping from my window,
Kissing my cheeks
Inviting me to stay in bed.

Clouds pour a blessing
As if trying to wash away all the pain
Another book is finally over
A new story awakes.

I will soar high to fulfill
 the pages of my new novel
like how the rain
 nurture the earth.

DUST

I want to recite a poem for my country

Compose lyrics that are true

But to touch the heart of stone

Needs words that seem toxic

For long, it can't be denied

There, yonder, here proliferated

Dust, strained my eyes

Caused grief and despair

All kinds of Dust

Counting them shattered my mind

All they gave was friction

Our lives dream burned by fire

But if we tolerate

How long can we endure?

dust in our society

Get up, act fast

Don't just suffer

Hurry up to the pinnacle
Suppress the dust.

Wrong acts, l we begin to forego
Follow the right path
Using everything we've got
To dedicate a victory to our Motherland.

You, I, We can do our best
Holding hands we show that we understand
We renounce the Dust
And our countrymen's resentment will subside.

Not easy, not difficult
Let's prepare our future
Strive hard to reach our dreams
Betterment is in the offing.

Let us unite for our nation's heritage
Friends, fellow countrymen
Never forget to pray to God
To instil peace in our hearts and minds.

KEY OF HAPPINESS

Being far from my loved ones

Separated by borders and oceans

Here in the foreign land, I learned how to dance

And face the life full of endurance

When my cheeks glazing with rain

Nothing can ease the pain

But my phone full of memories inside

Deep in my heart will always reside

Living alone with my phone

My only way of connection

I can see what's going on

How my children are grown

Phone bind us together

Though far apart, still, I can show I care

Letting them feel I will always be there

No matter what, a father is here

Seeing the smiles, listening to their laughter

It gave me the strength to become stronger

When sleep nowhere to find

On the screen, there's peace of mind.

So please allow me to use my phone

For it is my only way to reach home.

SO NEAR

Though the sun scorching my skin

I can see the smile of the heaven

Reminding me to stay calm

And just keep going

I'm already far from where I've been

Struggles may come and disturb me

Just like those clouds

But the sun can't dry my dreams

It's a strength to my muscle

To my sweat, I am willing to shower

I can smell it from the air

Success it whispers

It's very near.

I DO

Respect each other with humane and just

Because how we cover ourselves doesn't define us

I love wearing a fitted dress,

It makes me feel sexy

I like to use high heels,

I can walk confidently

Your opinion regarding my outfit

doesn't matter to me

I don't care what you think

I mind my own identity

I don't have oozing beauty

But I carry myself with dignity

Do you?

NOTHING

Nothing in life is free

Not even

Chances

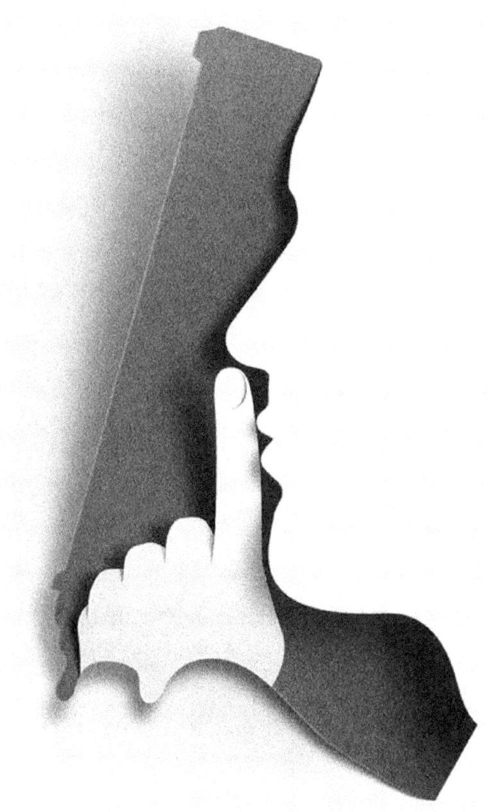

BEHIND MASK

Should I write my deepest thought
 under your skin, for you to understand
 my words?

Does anyone notice-
Silence isn't always a sign of ignoring nor a sign of
absence,
it can be the loudest scream of hidden pain.
Smiling is not always a sign of happiness,
it can be a sign of emptiness.

Does anyone notice if one star was missing out of
the sky?
Does anyone notice the rain behind the dark
clouds?

I notice between fake and real.
I notice the beauty in darkness.
I notice every truth behind the lies.
I notice you and me.
Broken but still shimmers.

UNICO IJO

In the middle of the night

When the darkness covered my eyesight

I felt your hand holding mine, hugging it tightly

Silently screaming "please don't leave me"

I controlled my emotion, kept and hide

Although there's a fire burning me inside

Like a spear, bull's eye to my heart

I knew it, you don't want us to be far apart

Yet I chose to leave you

Which I thought the best thing to do

Forgive me for letting you sleep in pain

One day I will be back, will never leave you again.

TOGETHER FOREVER

Looking back when we were young
You used to be soft-hearted
You were so fragile
They love to caress us
While singing lullaby
Until we fall asleep

As we grow older
We become stronger
We always hold each other
Interlocked like a zipper
Kissed each other while we offer our prayer

We used to comfort each other when one is in pain
A simple message on our vein
After carrying the heavy burden
I can see our shadow of yesterday
Scars of a hidden story
Marks of being clumsy
Reminding us to take extra care

But life challenged us

You started to make a fuss

You become a monster

Well, me too I guess!

We're like crazy

Paranoid really

Our friends act differently

Though we have the same identity

Treated us like an enemy

Relatives stay away from us

Never dare to say hi

When we beg for help, they resist

As if we have a contagious disease

We pretend we never notice

We learned how to play hide and seek.

I have you, you have me

We tried to live peacefully

Though our hearts filled with so much worry

We bathe very often

We took a hot shower

Learn to apply moisturizer

Sanitize every corner

To cleanse deep within

Washing off those unseen

We shall not be defeated

No time to be scared

You and I stick with each other together

Building our life for better

You and me on board

Fighting against the world.

HOLLOW

When everyday is ______day

I don't mind _____ until ____

because it's my ____ as your ____

but at least be _____. I am not _____

of ____, _____ and_____ but ______

of your unstoppable ______ mouth.

You said I'm_______ but who_____

your_____?

You said I'm_____ but who_______

your_____?

You said I'm______ but who_______

your_____?

I don't ask for more

I am a ______

So please treat me as a ______.

EMPAT PERKATAAN

virus attacks, Nanay worry

lagi praying, feeling sorry

butas pocket, empty wallet

remain hopeful, lifting the spirit

persist living, zero income

defeat trauma, lockdown tiresome

daily routine, doing nothing

lakad takbo makan sleeping

DAYDREAMING

Here I am, in front of the mirror
 dancing, smiling like a crazy witch,
  finally, they give what I ask for.
You see, I'm so excited (giggling)
 my special day has started
I saw lights, colourful lights
  dancing in the night.
Yeah, that's what I want.

Chairs and tables,
Flower arrangement all-around
 the total package of what I want.
 yeah, that's what I want.
It's my birthday, I'm eighteen
I want things to be count the same as my age
Soon I will be out of the cage.

La,la,la,la eighteen candles was there
to be lighted by female friends and cousins,
Yeah, that's what I want.
Eighteen red roses to be given one by one

and surely ask me to dance graciously.

Tuxedo for a male and lovely gown for female,

Yes, that's what I want.

Another eighteen in terms of wishing

mostly from my family and best friends

To write their wish in a balloon

and let it fly to the moon.

Yeah, that's what I want.

OH! Wait, wait, I can't believe it

just give me a minute

It's awesome, looks yummy

delicious, finger lick'n good...

Can you see, can you see

What my eyes see?

A big birthday cake, not used to be

Not just one layer but three

An answered prayer, I was so delightful

Cookies and cream, my tummy will surely fill.

Surrounded by different stuff

With stairs going on top

And there she is,

Statue of a princess.
Yeah, that's what I want.

Everything I want was there
Nothing more I could ask for.
The emcee calls for my name
"Come to the stage," he says.
Wearing my awesome gown,
I started to walk but suddenly
I feel someone shaking me.
I saw my mother looks irritably
and I heard from left to my right ear,
she shouts,
"You're dreaming, get up
you'll be late for school, lazy hmmph! "

COME AND GO

Arrived wearing the sweetest smile
    just like a glue that sticks into my face,
Thirst for your hug and love
 I surrendered my heart
 to feel your caress.
Every day shined like a diamond
as we spend a moment together
Full of joy, laughter's overload
You and I exactly fit in this world
Worth remembering, surely I treasured.
But hey, two weeks was so fast
 it ended just like that
Here I am
preparing to depart,
you and me once again
   far apart.
My legs are shaking
 heart is trembling
the smile covered with darkness
my face filled with tears
happiness goes to emptiness

but I have to continue
despite sorrow.

One day, I will come back
just wait patiently
and I pray for your desire
not to be weary and tire.

FIGHTING SPIRIT

I asked myself,
 should I try
or just
 simply don't mind
but you- you
keep on murmuring
telling me
to give a shot,
to show my line
and spread a rhyme.

after a day of
 thinking twice,
hesitance was set aside,
I decided to fight
though your thumb-up
 maybe out of sight.

Let's enjoy the ride,
poetry in the night
twinkling like a star

shining with a little light

you accept it or not

without notify,

still alright.

TWO FACES OF MIGRANT'S LIFE

She lived in two different worlds,
one is built with cement and rocks
surrounded with marbles and glass
spend a year or two of sacrifices,
courage is a must for all the hindrances.

After a year, she gets the chance
to meet the other face of her world,
A simple house not concrete nor big.
Yes, she's back in her mother's lap
She was welcome happily
with the warm embrace of love,
her delicious food readily served
favourite bedsheet wrapped her bed
lukewarm water for her to bathe
"take a full rest" as what her mother said.
Oh, how she wishes every day is like that, but she
knows it won't last.

In a blink of an eye, two weeks is over
she was back on the other side.

Just after she reached home from her flight,

she unpacked her luggage, but

a queen enforce her power,

"wash my car first, I need to go out"

"marketing tomorrow, we don't have food"

"later on, you clean the garage

many dry leaves from the plants"

"Tomorrow morning I want breakfast

make egg waffle, less butter less sweet."

Without a pause, without a no

she has to fulfill

what they requested to do

with a smile, seems still fine

D.H. you define.

That was her world

she was welcome

in two different ways

one with care and

one with power.

TREAT OR TRICK

There's nothing wrong with the helper's code.

 I can't believe that

They don't have a good life

They received a very unfair treatment

Is a big lie

Most helpers didn't suffer from depression

Twice a month a rest-day is enough for them

I disagree that

We have the right to complain

All the rules are part of the contract

It's not true that

Some of them need to go back at 5 pm to cook dinner

During day-off

Because, if you think carefully

We were treated fairly

And don't try to convince me that

Helpers suffered a lot.

NUCLEUS POEMS

1.

My love

You vanished, I'm waiting in vain

Happiness was embezzled by your absence

  and my heart tainted by pain

I wonder, will you ever come back again?

2.

I'm here

 Still alone in my shattered world

Trying to figure out how to fix the broken pieces

 into anew

I know, there's a rainbow after the rain.

3.

Those tears,

 Letting go of what is over

Throwing away all the unnecessary memories

  inside of me

One day, everything will be fine.

WHEN HEAVENS WEPT

Slowly, gently

Teasing a bit, sarcastic

When suddenly become angry

It sounds like a grenade that was exploded

With simultaneous flashing of fire

 Looks like a sword blade

that can divide me into two

Weight of feelings

Released immediately

Clouds drifting

Poured out rudely

It seems to be endless

While the clouds pouring rain

A shadow in the street wiping the sign of pain.

I RIDE

Without knowing the fruit of this journey

To chase dreams in the lion city

To follow the voice shouting from my head

Though I can hear the drum in my chest

I will keep riding

I will keep going

Like a bird in the sky

Soaring high

Despite the heavy burden

The wind is uncertain

Sometimes I'm out of balance

Yet reminding myself there's a second chance

I may turn in a wrong direction

Due to my blurry vision

But I won't give up

To reach on top.

WHEN I CAN'T USE "E"

Why would I twist my brain
Just to follow the ruling
Why would I insist on omitting
Taking away that crazy thing
I must admit, it's difficult
Looking back and forth
Finding what is wrong
As if I'm singing and got a gong
Looking for synonyms
Trying to fix my rhythm

In my mind, lots of thought running
I can't stop smiling
Why duck always quack, quack
And frog always ribbit or croak
Looking at dark clouds
Waiting for a colourful rainbow
It's hard but full of fun
As hard as cooking without salt,
washing my hair without shampoo,
digging mountain for gold.

Omitting is so tricky

As tricky as calligraphy

This is so intriguing

But a good training

Now should I sing humpty dumpty

Or shout for my victory?

AFTER A DECADE

Would it be ok to open my heart

to show your love engraved inside

Would it be ok to say you're always there at all cost

when I call your name and needed you most?

Would it be ok if I let the world know

we've been together for 10 years of high and low?

You always give so much of yourself unselfishly

Do you realize how much you mean to me?

Our love is about you and me

With our hearts intertwined for eternity

It's not about the chocolates or dozen of roses

It's the love you gave me, I am blessed

It's not about a promise "I'll give you the moon"

It's staying by my side despite the storm

It's not about giving expensive gifts

It's spending your time with me is the best.

I can paint your face even if I close my eyes

Your eyes that speaks a thousand words

Your mouth that you shut when I'm in a bad mood

You never argue, you don't insist your side

You'll wait until the fire in me subside

I may be the most impossible person

But you love me despite my different seasons.

Thank you for a decade of love

It was never easy, yet you didn't give up

After all the storms we faced, I can still say

You're the man who made my day

Because of your love

I always survive

Are we meant to last?

In God we trust.

FORGIVE ME

I know it wasn't easy
 Growing up without me
 I didn't mean to hurt you such
Just remember that
I love you so much
and I'm doing whatever that I could
to give you all the best in this world.

I decided to go to another country
 to work and earn enough money.
Hoping it is the right decision
 to save money for your education.
I recall the day when I am leaving,
inside of me seems dying.
You cried while you hold the layers of my dress...
It breaks my heart...
It breaks my heart to see you in tears.
My heart seems to shatter.
I don't know what to say.
I don't know what to do to ease your pain.
 You shall not live in vain.

I can see the sadness in your eyes, and all can do...

all I do is kiss and hug you tight.

I smile at you as if I am fine

Still wave my hand as a sign of goodbye.

Trying to control my feeling

 Not to show you I'm crying

I'm sorry if I'm leaving.

Inside the airplane I let it go,

 I cried as if no tomorrow.

I will be missing you;

I love you, I really do

Every night, the pain moves into my eyes

 Dreaming...

Wishing you're with me all the time.

Thinking of you makes me sad and unwell.

Forgive me

if I cant even teach you how to read and how to

write ABC;

If I cannot read to you your favourite book stories

 and watch your favourite show.

Forgive me

When you cried and I wasn't there to wipe your
tears;
When every night I wasn't there while you were
having a nightmare.
Forgive me when I can't hug you every time
 you were frightened by the lightning and thunder;
When you call my name and I can't be there.
Forgive me when you fall sick and I cannot show
you I care.
Forgive me when you fall and I'm nowhere to lift
you.
Forgive me when you need my help but I'm absent.
This is not for eternity, but only for a moment.

Forgive me I wasn't there to attend all school
meeting;
I wasn't there during the family day;
I wasn't there to cheer for you when you have to
perform in your school program;
I wasn't there to give you a big applause every time
you receive
 an award of being outstanding in class.
I'm far away from you.

But you study so hard to be on top.

I know it's tough from the very start

 to grow up without a mother by your side.

I'm sorry for taking this path but

I hope someday, my love you will grasp.

Please understand...

Please understand I was caught

in the middle of the dark.

But I will never give up

I will fight no matter what

I will stay on the right track

And one day,

when the right time comes,

In your arms...

I will be back.

WHISPER OF THE MIND

There's no one willing to listen, so here
I am, alone, sitting on the ground, searching
For what is hidden and unsaid.
I see the waves, stomping on the shore
As if trying to erase the footprints of yesterday.
The cold breeze kisses my cheeks like the gentle
Touch of my mother, comforting me when I'm sick.
The scents of the flowers scattered in the air
Like the love of my father, whose love
Is silent but strong.

I can't help but wonder…
How can the waves crash in so perfectly?
Maybe if it can erase all my heartaches
Then I should have written them on the sand,
Letting the waves bring them away, never to
return.
How can the sunlight shine so fiercely?
Like how fire bursts from an angry heart.
Is the wind dancing with the trees?

110

Or is she testing their roots?

Like how problems test my patience.

How can those flowers blossom so beautifully?

Are they destined to make butterflies and bees

happy?

Or like you and me, destined to see each other only

for a moment,

Parting ways because we choose diverging paths?

Dominating ocean where the clouds have sunken

While blue curtains silently cover the heavens,

Those birds flying free in the sky

Remind me that to achieve my dreams

I must soar high.

All around me, nature is alive and sparkling,

While I'm here sitting on the ground,

Holding my knees to my chest.

Here I am, hoping one day, just like the sea,

I too can showcase my best.

(This poem with its Tagalog version appeared in The
Tiger Moth Eco Journal)

ABOUT THE AUTHOR

Originally from the Island of Marinduque, the heart of the Philippines, **Rea Maac** has been working in Singapore since 2010. Her poem "Alikabok" was shortlisted for the Migrant Workers Poetry Competition 2016 and was included in the anthology Songs from a Distance. She also contributed to the books Our Homes, Our Stories: Voices of Migrant Domestic Workers in Singapore, and Call and Response: A Migrant/Local Poetry Anthology. Her also poems appeared in Journals and e-book like The Tiger Moth Eco Journal and

Translating Migration: Multilingual Poems of Movement.